LUANNA AND THE KIDS' COURT
The Doll Dilemma

CARON PESCATORE

Cover art by Jeanine Henning

ISBN-10: 0997587903

ISBN-13: 978-0997587906

Library of Congress Control Number: 2016907255

LCCN Imprint Name: Brixton Books, Marshfield MA

Printed in the United States of America

For God,
without whom this book could not have been written;
for my husband,
who pushed, cajoled, and encouraged me;
and for my children,
who were constant sources of inspiration.

CHAPTER 1

A Great Idea!

"THAT'S NOT FAIR!"

Luanna Porcello looked up just in time to see Jennifer Corbett come storming out of the front door of her house. Following directly behind her was her twin brother, Jimmy.

"I tell you, Jen, I didn't do it!" he exclaimed.

"And I say you did," Jenny shot back as she took off running across their front yard.

Jimmy walked dejectedly toward where Luanna stood; his head was down, shoulders drooped. He was a small, slender youth, with spindly arms and legs, wavy brown hair, and light-blue eyes that were enlarged to the size of saucers behind his thick-rimmed glasses. Jimmy invariably had an air of distraction about him. He was extremely bright, and his mind seemed always to be elsewhere. He was quite the junior inventor, and if he wasn't actually involved in creating a new invention, he was thinking about one.

"Hey, Jimmy, what's up?" Luanna asked. She was a tall, slender girl, with dark-brown hair and amber-colored eyes.

Jimmy looked up, an expression of surprise on his face. "Oh, hi, Lulu. I didn't see you standing there." He sighed. "Rebecca was destroyed. Someone tore her head off. Jenny's convinced it was me, but it wasn't! She's angry because Mom and Dad believe me and refused to make me pay for it." Rebecca was Jenny's prized Glamour Girl doll.

"Oh, that's terrible!" Luanna exclaimed. She knew just how much Jenny loved Rebecca. In addition to that, the doll was extremely expensive. "How do you think that happened?"

"I don't know," Jimmy responded. "The head was ripped off, and it's missing."

Just then Jenny walked up. In appearance she was very similar to her twin—minus the glasses—but in temperament the two couldn't have been more different. While Jimmy was quiet and studious, Jenny had a bubbly, outgoing personality, and no one could ever accuse her of being bookish. "What are you doing, Jimmy?" she asked her brother. "Confessing your crime to Lulu?"

"I told you," Jimmy fumed, "I had nothing to do with destroying your doll!"

"That's what you say, but I know differently."

"I don't know why you're so determined to believe I broke your doll."

"Maybe it's because you're always breaking my toys testing your stupid inventions," Jenny replied.

"I won't deny I've broken a few of your toys during my experiments," Jimmy admitted, "but that's in the past. I promised Mom and Dad I wouldn't do that anymore, and I haven't. Besides, I know how much you love Rebecca. I would never hurt her!"

Jenny stuck her nose in the air and sniffed. "I don't believe you!"

Jimmy sighed. "I wish there was some way I could prove to you that I didn't do it."

"And I wish there was some way I could prove that you did. Then Mom and Dad would make you pay for Becky."

During their exchange Luanna had remained silently listening. She hated seeing the siblings fight. Usually they were extremely close, as was typically the case with twins. As she listened to them argue, an idea suddenly came to her. "Guys, I think there's a way you can prove what really happened to Jenny's doll!" she exclaimed.

Jenny and Jimmy turned toward her.

"What are you thinking, Lulu?" Jimmy asked.

Jenny eyed her suspiciously. "Why should I trust you? You probably think Jimmy's telling the truth and only want to prove he's innocent."

Luanna smiled. "It won't matter what I think. Because my idea is this: we take your case to court!"

"Court!" the twins exclaimed.

"How would we do that?" Jimmy asked.

"Yeah," Jenny added. "What court is going to listen to our case?"

Luanna smiled. "A kids' court. A court made up by kids for kids."

Both siblings looked at Luanna as though she'd lost her mind.

"We can have a judge, lawyers, a bailiff—everything just like a real court!" she continued excitedly. "It will be great!"

"I'm not sure," Jimmy said doubtfully.

"Well," Luanna replied, "my dad says there's no better way to find the truth in any situation than by going to court."

The twins looked impressed. All the neighborhood kids knew that Luanna's dad was a successful prosecutor with the district attorney's office. So if he said going to court was the best way to find the truth, then that was good enough for them.

"OK," Jenny said. "You've sold me on the idea."

"Me, too," Jimmy added. "What do we need to do?"

"Well," Luanna responded, "first we need to gather up some of the other kids and see who wants to participate. We're going to need a few people if my plan is going to work. Let's meet at the fort after lunch, OK?"

"OK," the twins agreed.

❖ ❖ ❖

"Hey, Mom," Luanna called out as she ran through the back door of her house.

"Hey, you," her mother replied. "Perfect timing. Rosie is just about to put lunch on the table." Rosie—short for Rosalie—was the family's longtime housekeeper. "What have you been up to all morning?" Renee Porcello was a pretty woman of Jamaican descent, with dark-brown hair and eyes and light-brown skin.

"I hung out at Phoebe's," Luanna replied, referring to her best friend, Phoebe Chen.

Just as they were about to sit down to eat, Luanna's father walked in. "Hey, Dad, what are you doing here?" Luanna exclaimed.

David Porcello was a tall, well-built man, with wavy dark hair, hazel eyes, and a light-olive complexion. It was a surprise to see him at home in the middle of the day. As a senior prosecutor, he was always very busy at work. "I snuck out of the office so I could have lunch with my two best girls." He kissed his wife on the cheek. "But shh, it's a secret." His eyes twinkled with mischief as he tugged on one of Luanna's long braids. She giggled.

After the three had said grace and settled down to eat, Luanna told her parents about her idea for a kids' court.

"I think that's a great idea," her father said. "There is no better way to get at the truth than having an unbiased person look at all the evidence from both sides and make a decision."

"I agree," Mrs. Porcello added. Renee was also an attorney. She had her own private practice in partnership with another lawyer.

Luanna had spent a lot of time at both her parents' offices and watching them during their appearances in court. She found it all very fascinating and had decided she too wanted to be a lawyer when she grew up.

"The kids and I are meeting at the fort after lunch. We need to figure out how we're going to set up the court," she told her parents.

"Hmm," David Porcello said. "First you have to decide what type of court you're going to have—criminal or civil."

Luanna knew that in criminal cases, a person was charged with a crime and, if found guilty, could be made to pay a fine or even be put in jail as punishment. On the other hand, civil cases typically involved one person suing another for money. "Civil, I think. I can't imagine that Jimmy needs to fear losing his freedom if he's found guilty." She giggled and added, "Although I'm sure Jen would love to have him locked away forever, if it's proved that he did destroy Rebecca."

"Well, you'll need a judge," her mother said. "And you should have a bailiff." A bailiff was the sheriff's deputy who was assigned to a court to keep order in the courtroom.

"Yes," her father agreed. "Plus you'll need an attorney for each side as well as a court reporter." A court reporter was the person who typed everything that was said in court. "You have to make sure you get an accurate record of everything that takes place in the courtroom."

"Hmm, and a jury, of course," Mrs. Porcello added. "Since it's a civil case, you'll need only six jurors."

Luanna groaned. That was a lot of people. During the summer a number of the neighborhood kids were either away at camp or on vacation with their families. "I don't know if we have that many kids available!"

"You could always have a bench trial," her father suggested.

"You mean a trial where the judge listens to both sides and decides the case instead of a jury?" Luanna asked.

"Exactly!" he replied as he looked at his watch. "Well, I'm off. I'm due in court in thirty minutes." After giving Luanna and her mom each a kiss, he left the room.

"I have to go too, Mom," Luanna said. "I'm meeting the others at the fort."

"Have fun, dear," Mrs. Porcello replied. "I have to meet a client at the office this afternoon. Be good for Rosie."

"Aren't I always?" Luanna asked. "See you later!"

CHAPTER 2

What's My Role?

ON HER WAY to the fort, Luanna stopped by Phoebe's house to take her along to the court meeting. Phoebe lived on Ferndale Road, which was the next street over from Luanna's. Her house was two doors down, on the opposite side of the road from the Corbetts' home. Her yard also conveniently abutted the conservation land on which the fort was located. As the two girls walked along, Luanna brought her friend up to speed.

"Oooh, a kids' court is a great idea, Lulu!" Phoebe enthused, her brown eyes sparkling with excitement. She was petite, with straight black hair and pale, creamy-gold skin.

Suddenly a large golden retriever went streaking by. In his mouth he carried a boot. As he disappeared among the trees on the conservation property, little Andrew Colton came running up.

"Have you seen Rufus?" he gasped. "He stole my dad's work boot!"

"He went running off that way," Phoebe responded, motioning toward the area where Rufus had disappeared.

"Thanks," Andrew replied. He took off running in the direction Phoebe had indicated.

"That dog is a menace!" Phoebe fumed. Luanna laughed. Phoebe glared at her. "It's easy for you to laugh," she huffed. "You don't have to worry about the mangy beast chewing up your stuff! Just last week he took off with Penelope's flute. I had to chase the wretched animal all the way to the other side of the fort. He was in the middle of burying it when I caught up to him. Luckily I caught him before he got the job done. Ugh!" Phoebe's sister, Penelope, was an accomplished flutist and had even earned a music scholarship to attend college in the coming fall. Her flute was her most prized possession.

Within minutes the girls arrived at the fort. It was a large clearing that was enclosed within a circle of trees and was completely hidden from view by a heavy undergrowth of bushes. It was very secluded, which explained why the older neighborhood kids had started referring to it as "the fort." The name had stuck through the years.

Upon their arrival Luanna and Phoebe discovered several kids waiting for them. In addition to the Corbett twins, there were three other children: Mary Beth Stover, a pretty blonde with deep-blue eyes; Jake Crandall, a tall, husky boy with reddish-blond hair that invariably had strands sticking out in all directions; and Lindsey Harrison, a quiet girl with dark-brown skin and hair, and light-gray eyes. At ten years of age, Lindsey was a year younger than the others. Besides Luanna she was the only one present who did not live on Ferndale Road. She, like Luanna, lived on Birch Street. Her house was directly across from the Porcello residence. As soon as Luanna and Phoebe arrived, the kids got down to business.

"What's this about you starting a kids' court, Lulu?" Jake Crandall abruptly demanded. Jake had a naturally loud voice and a somewhat forceful manner when he spoke. Add to that his large size, and he made for a very intimidating presence. For all his gruff exterior, however, he was a really sweet kid. He was fiercely loyal to his friends and could always be counted on to lend a helping hand whenever someone was in need of one.

"Well, Jake, I thought it might be a good idea to start one to help Jimmy and Jenny figure out the truth about what really happened to Jen's doll."

"What's there to figure out?" Jake asked. "Jimmy said he didn't touch her doll. And if Jimmy says he didn't do it, then that's good enough for me!"

Jake and Jimmy had been best friends pretty much since birth. They made an odd couple, to be sure. Jimmy was soft-spoken, scholarly, and very smart while Jake was loud, did his best to avoid anything to do with books, and wasn't exactly what one would call bright. His devotion to Jimmy, however, was unswerving, and over the years he'd saved his bookish friend from unscrupulous bullies time and again. By now everyone at school knew not to mess with Jimmy—not unless they wanted to deal with Jake.

"And I say he did do it!" Jenny chimed in.

Jake rolled his eyes at her. "Please. You just want Jimmy to pay for your precious doll. You know he didn't do it."

"I do not!"

Luanna sighed. Getting this group to settle down and work together was not going to be an easy task.

"Please you guys, let's not argue. The entire reason for starting a court is so we can find the truth without fighting."

"Let's get on with it," Jimmy said. "What do we need to do, Lu?"

"First we need to decide who's going to do what. We need a judge, lawyers for both parties, a bailiff, and a court reporter to start. Then, of course, we're going to need a jury, unless we decide to have a bench trial."

"Could you please speak English?" Jake grumbled. "You lost me. I get that we need a judge and lawyers, but what's this about a party? Will we need music? And what on earth is a bailiff?"

"Not *a* party, Jake. Parties. The parties in a case are the plaintiff and defendant. The plaintiff is the person who is bringing the complaint, while the defendant is the person who is defending against it." At Jake's blank expression, Luanna sighed again. "In our case Jenny says Jimmy broke her doll. In court she is the plaintiff, the one who is bringing the complaint. Jimmy is the defendant; he is the person who is accused of doing something wrong."

"So Jenny is a complainer," Jake said. "That's nothing new." Jenny glared at him. He continued, "And Jimmy is the defendant. I got that, but who are the other people you mentioned, and *what* is a bailiff?"

"A bailiff is a sheriff's deputy who is assigned to a courtroom to keep the peace. He protects the judge and makes sure everyone obeys the judge's rules."

"That's me!" Jake exclaimed. "I'm going to be the bailiff. Do I get to carry a gun? I can bring my MX 5!" The MX 5 was the latest addition to Jake's extensive toy gun collection.

"Um, Jake," Luanna interrupted, "I think your MX is a little on the large side. The bailiff carries a…a…a…" She looked helplessly at Jimmy.

"I think what Luanna is trying to say, Jake, is that the court deputy carries a handgun," Jimmy explained.

"Oh, I see." Jake looked crushed, but then his demeanor brightened. "So I can't use my new MX 5, so what? At least I get to carry a gun!" He beamed at the thought.

"Er, yes," Luanna responded. "Now for the other people we'll need for our court. We already have our plaintiff and defendant, of course. That's Jenny and Jimmy. We'll need two lawyers, one to represent each of them."

"I'll be Jenny's lawyer," Mary Beth piped up. "I think I can do a good job, Jen," she said to her friend.

"You know how obsessed my mom is with those courtroom drama television shows. I watch them with her all the time…Well, the ones she'll let me watch." She rolled her eyes. "She says most of them have inappropriate content." She lifted her hands and did the quotes gesture as she said the last two words.

Jenny nodded her head in agreement. "Mary Beth is my lawyer," she told Luanna.

"I want Luanna to be my lawyer," Jimmy said.

"Maybe Luanna should be the judge," a quiet voice interjected. All heads turned toward Lindsey. She had such an unassuming personality that oftentimes it was easy to forget she was even present. "After all," she continued, "a kids' court was her idea."

"Lindsey has a point," Phoebe agreed. "Besides, you're the one who knows the most about courts and legal stuff, Lulu. You must have spent half your childhood at your parents' offices and in real court!"

"True," Luanna agreed. "But to be honest, I'd rather be a lawyer. Why don't you be the judge, Lindsey?"

Lindsey's eyes opened wide in horror. "Me? Oh no! I couldn't! I'm not the judge type at all," she protested. The others silently agreed. Lindsey barely spoke above a whisper most times and had a very sweet but very timid personality. "I can be the court reporter," she offered. "I'm a pretty fast typist, and I can record everything on my laptop."

"That's great, Lindsey," Luanna replied. She looked at Phoebe. "How about you, Phoebs? Any interest in being the judge?"

"Nuh uh. I'd rather be Jimmy's lawyer."

"OK," Luanna agreed reluctantly. "But before I agree to be the judge, let's see if we can get someone else to do it. Also, we're going to need a jury, but I'm thinking we might have to do a bench trial."

"There she goes, speaking Greek again," Jake complained. "What is this bench trial you keep talking about? Do we all need to sit on benches or something?"

"No, Jake." Luanna laughed. "A bench trial is one where the judge listens to all the evidence and decides the outcome." Jake looked at her quizzically. Luanna smiled. "The judge decides who wins. In a jury trial, there's a jury of either six or twelve people who decide the winner."

"Why can't we have a jury trial?" Jenny demanded. "Seems to me it would be better to have six people decide instead of one. I mean, that's a lot of power to give one person. And besides, no offense, Luanna, but I'm not sure I want *you* making that decision. Everyone knows you have a soft spot for Jimmy."

It was true. Luanna had a particular fondness for Jimmy. They shared a mutual love of books and learning and over the years had voluntarily partnered together on countless school projects.

"The problem is," Luanna replied, "there aren't that many kids around right now."

"That's true," Lindsey added softly. "The Hasanis, Newmans, and Castillos are away on vacation."

"Yeah," added Jake, "and the Foster boys and Declan Mathias have day camp all this week."

"Hmm, that doesn't leave a lot of kids to choose from," Jimmy observed.

"Actually there's no one else to choose from," Phoebe corrected, "unless you want to have a jury made up of four-, five-, and six-year-olds."

"Absolutely not!" Jenny declared. "I don't want a bunch of babies deciding my case."

"Well, that leaves us with only one option," Luanna observed. "We'll have to have a bench trial."

"What about my sister, Heather?" Jake asked. "Maybe we can convince her to be the judge. She's not friends with either Jimmy or Jenny, so she wouldn't care who wins. She'll be a pain to put up with, though. Ever since she turned thirteen on her last birthday, she thinks she's soooo cool!"

"Heather is a great idea, Jake!" Jenny enthused. "I think we should ask her."

"I agree," Jimmy added. "If Heather agrees to be the judge, then Luanna can be my lawyer."

"OK, great!" Luanna was excited. "Let's ask her right away, so we can get started."

"Ahem. Excuse me." Everyone turned to look at Phoebe. "Haven't you forgotten something?"

"Um, I don't think so," Luanna replied. "*Did* I forget something?"

"What about me?" Phoebe demanded. "Now that you're Jimmy's lawyer, what part am I going to play in this little courtroom drama, assuming, of course, Heather agrees to be the judge?"

"Oh, Phoebs, I'm so sorry!" Luanna felt terrible. "Why don't you help me represent Jimmy? You could indulge your Nancy Drew fantasy and be my private investigator," she added temptingly.

Phoebe's eyes gleamed. There was nothing she liked better than solving puzzles. In this way she was very much like her father, Robert Chen, who was the chief of detectives at the Oakdale Police Department. He often told Phoebe that working a case was very much like solving a puzzle. Phoebe had always thought it would be awesome to solve mysteries like her father—or Nancy Drew. "Oh, perfect! I've always wanted to be a detective!"

"Works for me," Jimmy responded. "But what exactly will you be doing?"

"Yeah," Mary Beth piped up, "and how come Jimmy gets to have a private investigator, but Jenny doesn't?"

"Mary Beth's right. It doesn't seem fair," Jenny interjected.

"Let's not argue, guys," Luanna said. "Of course Jenny can have a private investigator on her team if she wants one. Just find someone who will agree to do it."

"Good. I'll ask Ashley," Mary Beth said, referring to her nine-year-old sister. "She'll do it. She likes watching Mom's courtroom drama shows almost as much as I do."

"OK, now that we have that settled, let's go get ourselves a judge!" Phoebe exclaimed.

CHAPTER 3

You Be The Judge

"WHAT DO YOU children want?" Heather Crandall demanded. She was a tall, gangling girl, with curly, red hair, pale skin, and freckles; she wore lime-green braces on her teeth.

"Um...er...Heath," Jake stammered, "we need a favor of sorts."

"And why would I do anything for you lot?" his sister questioned.

"It's like this, Heather," Luanna interjected. "We're starting a kids' court to solve a problem, but we're in need of someone to be the judge."

"Yeah," Phoebe chimed in, "but not just anyone can be the judge. The person needs to be firm but fair and highly intelligent. Jake thought you'd be the perfect candidate!" She gave Heather a wide-eyed, innocent look.

"He did, did he?" Despite her scathing tone, Heather looked intrigued. "Tell me more about this kids' court and what exactly I would be doing as the judge. Assuming I agree to do it, of course."

For the next half hour, the kids told Heather all about the children's court. In particular, they highlighted how important the judge's role would be and how perfectly suited she was for the position. There was nothing Heather Crandall liked more than having her ego pampered.

"All right, I'll do it," she announced after they had given her all the details. "When do we start?"

"The sooner the better, I would think," Luanna replied. "How about tomorrow morning, right after breakfast?"

All the kids nodded in agreement.

"But where are we going to hold court?" Lindsey asked. "We can't exactly have it at the fort. It's a little too uncomfortable, don't you think?"

"Good point," Luanna agreed. "Hmm, I think we can do it in my basement. I'm sure my parents wouldn't mind if we used one of the empty rooms down there."

"Sounds good!" Jake exclaimed. He rubbed his hands together. "I can't wait to get started. All of you better be on your best behavior, or I'll toss you out on your ears!"

"Hmm, isn't it for the judge to decide who gets tossed out of court?" Heather queried.

Jake gave her a disgruntled look. "You aren't going to spend the entire time bossing me around, are you?" he asked.

"Just you make sure you behave, or *I'll* toss *you* out of court!" Heather informed him. Turning to the others, she said, "I'll see you all tomorrow." They all said their good-byes and left.

❖ ❖ ❖

The next morning all the kids gathered in the Porcellos' basement. A major portion of the area consisted of a huge library, den, and workout room. So far, however, Luanna's parents were undecided as to what to do with the rest of the space. There was one room that originally had been intended as an office for Mrs. Porcello's use when she worked from home, but she had decided she preferred to work in the library or the upstairs study. Consequently, the room remained empty. It was to this room that Luanna led the group of children.

"Mom said we could use this room. She also said we're welcome to use any of the old furniture we find stored down here."

"Awesome!" Jake exclaimed.

"It's a nice size room," Heather commented, looking around at the space. It was a fairly large room with several windows and two doors—one that led out into the rest of the basement and another that led directly to the outside. "I like the fact that there's a door that leads outside. That way we won't bother your parents with our comings and goings."

Luanna chuckled. "Actually, Rosie said something about that too. She's happy we won't be trampling dirt throughout her clean house!"

"We should probably get to work, huh?" Phoebe suggested. "Where's the furniture your parents have stored down here?"

"There's a storage room on the other side of the basement," Luanna replied.

The kids all headed down the hallway to raid the storage closet. When they arrived Heather quickly claimed an old, battered desk as her own. "This will make a great desk for a judge, don't you think?" she asked Luanna.

"Yeah," Luanna agreed. "And it's actually called a bench."

"I think you're losing it, Luanna," Jake said. "That is most definitely not a bench. It's a desk."

Luanna laughed. "I didn't mean that, Jake. I meant that where the judge sits in court is called a bench."

"Oh. Why?" he asked.

Luanna shrugged. "I'm not sure. I guess it's because it's long and kind of resembles a bench, except you sit behind it instead of on it."

"Well, whatever it's called," Heather said, "I'm taking it for myself. Gimme a hand getting this down to the courtroom," she said to Jake. He moved to help her while the other kids got to work going through the rest of the furniture in the storage room.

Within an hour they had moved several pieces to the room and set it up to resemble a real court as much as they could. Heather's desk was placed at the front, facing the rest of the room. Lindsey had claimed a small kids' table with a matching chair as her own. This was placed next to Heather's desk, on her right. When sitting, Lindsey too would face the courtroom. To use as counsel tables, the kids had snagged two folding tables, one for the defense and one for the plaintiff. These were placed side by side in the middle of the room, facing Heather's and Lindsey's desks.

❖ **27** ❖

In between the two tables was an old audio-visual cart that was adjustable in height. Luanna thought it was the perfect piece to serve as a lectern where the attorneys could put their notes and other papers while questioning witnesses. To use as seats, the kids had taken several folding chairs. They had also placed a row of chairs directly behind the two counsel tables, where potential jurors, witnesses, and visitors to the court could sit. Jake had placed a chair on one side of the room. It was his contention that he should be in a position where he could "keep an eye" on everyone and make sure they weren't "trying to cause trouble." While testifying, witnesses would sit facing the rest of the courtroom in an empty chair that was located to the left of Heather's desk.

"OK, now that we've got everyone where they ought to be, we should probably get started, don't you think?" Heather asked.

"Yes, that's a good idea," Luanna agreed.

"Wait," Jake interjected. "Shouldn't Heather have one of those hammer things that judges use all the time?"

"Oh, you mean a gavel," Luanna said. She thought about it for a moment. "My dad gave me a toy one a few years ago. I think I still have it somewhere. Wait a sec." With that she ran out of the room. A few minutes later, she returned, waving a small wooden object in her hand triumphantly. "Here it is!"

"Thanks," Heather said as Luanna handed her the gavel. "Before we begin, Luanna, maybe you could give us an overview of how we should do things," she suggested.

"OK," Luanna replied. "Hmm, let me see. Well, when we're ready to begin, you say, 'Court is in session.' Then, when we're taking a break, you say, 'Court is in recess,' or 'Court is adjourned.' Because Jenny is the plaintiff, she gets to go first. She has the burden of proof. In other words it's up to her to convince you that Jimmy is guilty. In order to do that, she must prove her case by a preponderance of the evidence."

"A what of who?" Jake asked.

"A preponderance of the evidence," Luanna repeated. "That means she has to prove it's more likely than not that Jimmy is guilty. Think of it as a fifty-one/forty-nine percent split. She has to prove that it's fifty-one percent likely that he is guilty."

"How would she do that?" Heather questioned.

"She can bring in any evidence she has that proves her claim that Jimmy broke her doll. That evidence can include witness testimony as well as any items she may have. For example, if she had a picture of Jimmy breaking her doll, she would be allowed to bring that to court as proof." Luanna giggled. "Of course if she had such a picture, we wouldn't need a court."

"What's this witness test...test...um, what you just said?" Jake asked.

"A witness is someone who comes to court to give evidence," Luanna explained. "In other words witnesses tell what they know about the issue that is being decided. The witness is sworn in—that means he or she promises to tell the truth. The lawyers then get to ask the witness questions. When the witness speaks or answers questions, it's called testifying."

She looked around at her friends to make sure everyone was onboard with what she was saying; she then continued, "In our case Jenny can bring in witnesses to testify on her behalf, and she herself can testify. When a lawyer questions his own witness, it's called a direct examination, and when he questions a witness who was brought to court by the other party, it's a cross-examination."

"What about me?" Jimmy questioned. "What do I have to do to prove I'm innocent?"

"Actually, Jimmy, you don't have to prove you're innocent. The burden of proof is on Jenny. That means it's her job to prove you're guilty. Of course if you have any evidence to show you aren't guilty, you're allowed to bring it to court. You too can bring in witnesses and other evidence, and you can also testify on your own behalf.

"Any evidence that is brought into court must be authenticated. That means a person must testify as to what the item is and how it relates to the case. Once an item is produced in court, it is given an identifying number or letter and admitted into evidence. That means the court takes possession of it until the case is over. In our case we could label evidence from the plaintiff as A, B, and C, and evidence from the defense as one, two, three, and so on."

"OK, I think we have a pretty good idea of what we're supposed to be doing," Heather said as she glanced around at all the faces at the table. "What about court rules, Luanna? Are there any we should know about?"

"Well, there's basic stuff, such as don't interrupt when another person is talking, never argue with the judge, the judge gets the final word, and so on. Absolutely never speak when the judge is speaking. Also, you should always address the judge as Your Honor, and stand when speaking to the Court or questioning a witness. Anything you have to say should be said to the Court...the judge being the Court. In other words if I have something to say to Mary Beth, I don't speak to her directly but would speak to Heather, who is the Court. And we should call one another by our last names. You know, Miss Porcello, Miss Chen, and so on."

"All righty then," Heather said. "Let's get started. "Mary Beth, as Jenny's lawyer, you get to start. Are you ready?"

"Yes, we're ready," Mary Beth replied.

"OK, everyone, court is now in session," Heather announced, banging the gavel on the table. Ashley giggled, earning herself a warning glance from Heather. "The case we're here to decide is Jennifer Corbett versus James Corbett. Miss Corbett claims Mr. Corbett destroyed her Glamour Girl doll by ripping off its head. Mr. Corbett denies her claim. Miss Stover, you may begin."

Mary Beth stood up and moved to stand at the lectern. "Thank you, Your Honor. Jenny—I mean, Miss Corbett—will be my first witness," she said.

"Please come forward, Miss Corbett, and sit in the witness chair." Heather indicated the chair on her left. "Bailiff, please swear in the witness."

Jake stepped forward, chest puffed out with importance. "Please raise your right hand," he directed. Jenny raised her hand. "Do you promise to tell the truth, the whole truth, and nothing but the truth?"

"I do."

"Thank you, Officer Crandall," Heather said. "You may begin, Miss Stover."

"Miss Corbett, do you know the, um...what is Jimmy called again?" Mary Beth asked, turning to look at Luanna.

"I'm sorry, I don't understand your question," Luanna responded.

"I mean he's the one who Jenny says did something wrong; that makes him the...?"

"Oh, he's the defendant."

"Oh yes, that's it. Thanks. Miss Corbett, do you know the defendant, James Corbett?"

"Yes, I do."

"How is it that you know him?"

"He's my brother."

"Um...how long have you known him?"

"All of my life."

"All of your life. I see." Mary Beth paused then asked, "And, er—how long has that been?"

"I'm eleven, so that means I've known him eleven years."

"Umm, do you—do you live together?"

"Yes, we do."

Sitting next to Luanna, Phoebe began to fidget.

Mary Beth continued, "And...and how long have you—er—lived together?"

"All of our lives."

"I...see," Mary Beth said slowly. "Um...ah...how—how long has that been?"

Jenny frowned. "Eleven years."

Phoebe smothered a laugh. Luanna looked at her and made a soft *shh* sound.

Mary Beth furrowed her brow but didn't say anything. The silence dragged on for a full minute before Heather spoke up.

"Miss Stover, are you...finished?" she inquired.

"Um...no, Your Honor. I'm sorry, I was just trying to gather my thoughts," Mary Beth replied. "I'm ready with my next question."

"That's good," Heather replied. "You may continue."

"Miss Corbett—er—Miss Corbett...how—how long—um—how long has the defendant known you?" Mary Beth asked.

Phoebe burst out laughing. Mary Beth turned to glare at her. "Phoebe Chen, you stop laughing this instant!" she commanded. "I'd like to see you try to do this."

"I'm sorry! I'm sorry," Phoebe gasped. She bent her head over her knees and continued to laugh.

"Order in the court!" Heather ordered, banging the gavel on her desk several times in a row. "Miss Chen, pull yourself together, or I'll have the bailiff remove you from my courtroom!"

"I'm sorry, Your Honor," Phoebe spluttered. She looked apologetically at Mary Beth.

"This is harder than it looks on TV," Mary Beth huffed. "I'm not even sure what I'm supposed to be asking."

"You're right, Mary Beth," Luanna agreed. "It is harder than it looks. And as the plaintiff's lawyer, you have the difficult job of proving her case against Jimmy."

"How do I do that?" Mary Beth asked.

"You started out very nicely, I thought," Luanna told her kindly. "You established a relationship between Jenny and Jimmy, which is important. Now you need to prove the main elements of your case, which are that Jenny owns a Glamour Girl doll, that doll was destroyed, and Jimmy is the one who destroyed it.

"It will be necessary for you to bring in proof, such as Jenny's testimony, any witnesses you may have, and any other evidence. It might help if you wrote your questions down or at least a few notes, to remind yourself of the key points you want to bring out during your examination of each witness."

Mary Beth nodded her head. "I think I've got it." She looked at Heather. "Your Honor, would it be possible to take a short break so I can prepare a little? I know I said I was ready, but I think I wasn't really thinking about all I need to do."

"Of course," Heather responded. "Let's plan on returning after lunch, if that works for everybody?" She looked around at the others, who were all nodding their heads in agreement. "Good. I'll see you then. Court is adjourned."

CHAPTER 4

The Drama Begins

"HOW'S COURT GOING?" Rosie asked as Luanna and Phoebe came bouncing into the kitchen.

"Good," Luanna responded.

Phoebe giggled. "We actually didn't get very far," she said. "We ran into some unexpected difficulties."

Rosie raised her eyebrows in question. She was a tall, imposing woman, with dark-brown skin and warm, intelligent brown eyes. She, too, was from Jamaica and spoke with a lilting accent.

"Mary Beth was a little confused about what to do," Luanna elaborated. "She wasn't quite sure how to go about proving Jenny's case."

Rosie was familiar with all the details of the case, having listened to Luanna's excited chatter about the children's court the previous evening. "I'm sure you helped her figure things out," she said to Luanna.

"Yes, she did," Phoebe said. "But then Mary Beth asked for a break, so she could prepare. We're meeting up again after lunch."

"Speaking of lunch..." Rosie said. With that she started to move around the kitchen, preparing the girls' meal.

While they ate, Phoebe and Luanna discussed the case.

"How do you think Jenny is going to prove that Jimmy broke her doll?" Phoebe asked.

"I'm not sure," Luanna replied slowly. "I've been racking my brain all night thinking about that. It's not like she saw him do it, otherwise she would have told her parents."

"True," Phoebe agreed. The two friends descended into silence, each preoccupied with her own thoughts.

"However they go about proving it, we need to be prepared," Luanna finally said, breaking the silence.

"Yeah," Phoebe agreed, frowning. "We'd better be prepared for anything."

❖ ❖ ❖

When Mary Beth returned to court that afternoon, she was lugging a heavy-looking cardboard box in her arms.

"What's that?" Phoebe asked.

"You'll see," Mary Beth replied mysteriously.

Phoebe and Luanna exchanged glances. They wondered what trick Mary Beth had up her sleeve.

When Heather arrived, she immediately took her seat and banged the gavel. "Order in the court. Is everyone here?" she asked, looking around the room.

"Looks like we're all here, Your Honor," Luanna told her.

"Good, then let's get started." Heather banged the gavel on the judge's bench again. "Court is in session. Miss Stover, are you ready to proceed?"

"Yes, Your Honor. I call Miss Corbett to the witness chair."

Jenny sat in the witness chair. Heather looked at her, saying, "Now remember, Miss Corbett, you're still under oath."

"Yes, Your Honor."

"Miss Corbett," Mary Beth said, "you've accused the defendant, James Corbett, of destroying your

Glamour Girl doll. Has he ever broken any of your other toys before?"

"Yes, lots of times," Jenny replied.

"Can you tell us about some of those times?"

"Jimmy fancies himself something of a junior inventor. He's always coming up with new inventions, and then he has to test them to see if they work. One time he built this contraption. He said it was a rocket, but it didn't look like any rocket I'd ever seen. Anyway, he claimed he could use it to send objects to the moon."

"Did he ever test it to see if it would work?"

"Yes."

"What did he try to send to the moon?"

"He tried to send Ellie. She is—or, rather, I should say she *was*—my stuffed elephant."

"Why do you say she *was* your stuffed elephant?" Mary Beth questioned.

"Because his stupid invention didn't work!" Jenny exclaimed. "He strapped my poor Ellie to his so-called rocket, but when he tried to launch it, it blew up, and Ellie was blown to bits! All her stuffing went flying in every direction." Jenny looked as though she was ready to burst into tears.

Next to Luanna, Jimmy squirmed in his seat. "I said I was sorry, Jen. I never meant to hurt Ellie. I was sure my rocket would work!"

"Silence, Mr. Corbett," Heather barked. She underscored her order by banging the gavel on the bench. "You may continue, Miss Stover."

"Thank you, Your Honor." Mary Beth looked at Jennifer. "Miss Corbett, I know it must be dreadfully painful for you, having to relive this horrible event, but I have to ask you a few more questions."

"That's fine." Jenny sniffled and blew her nose on a tissue she had pulled out of her pocket. "I can continue."

Reaching inside the cardboard box she had brought into court, Mary Beth pulled out a small wooden box. "Your Honor, I'd like to have this item identified as Plaintiff's A."

"So marked," Heather responded.

Holding up the box, Mary Beth said, "Miss Corbett, do you recognize this item I'm holding in my hand?"

Jenny nodded. "I do."

"Could you please tell the Court what it is?"

"It's the box in which I keep Ellie."

"I'm sorry. I thought you said Ellie had been blown to bits."

"She was, but I collected all the pieces I could find and put them away in that box," Jenny explained. "Ellie was my best friend for nine years! I couldn't just throw her away!" She pulled out a clean tissue and dabbed at her eyes.

Mary Beth walked over and handed the box to Jennifer. "Could you please open the box and show the Court what's inside?"

Jenny did as she was told. She turned the box around, so the others could see its contents. Inside was a mass of white substance that looked almost exactly like cotton balls. Interspersed throughout were little pieces of light-gray material.

"I'm not sure how I'm supposed to record what's in the box," Lindsey said. Up until that point, she had been busily typing everything that was said on her laptop.

"Good point, Miss Harrison," Heather replied. "Any ideas, Miss Porcello?" she asked, looking at Luanna.

"You could instruct the witness to describe the contents, Your Honor," Luanna suggested.

"Good idea," Heather agreed. "Miss Corbett, please describe the contents of the box."

"Um, it's a lot of white cotton batting," Jenny said. "My mom told me that's what they called the material they used to stuff toys with a long time ago. Ellie was very old. She belonged to my grandmother, then to my mother, then to me. Now she's gone forever! And it's all his fault!" She lifted her hand and pointed a finger at her twin.

Heather rolled her eyes. *Kids*, she thought. *They are so dramatic.* "Pull yourself together, Miss Corbett." She looked at Mary Beth. "Do you have any more questions for this witness, Miss Stover?"

"Yes I do, Your Honor."

"Well, then, please continue," Heather directed.

Mary Beth continued with her questions. "Miss Corbett, tell us about another time when Mr. Corbett destroyed one of your toys."

"There was the time he cut off Miss Pig Pen's leg when he tried to invent a pair of 'baby-safe' scissors. Our brother, Colin, was a baby then, and he liked playing with scissors. He would cry for them whenever Jimmy or I was using them. Jimmy decided to come up with a way to blunt the edges of a pair, to make them safe for Colin to play with. *That* didn't work, and when he cut Miss Pig Pen's leg to demonstrate how safe they were, he cut it off!"

Reaching into the cardboard box, Mary Beth pulled out a toy pig that was missing its right leg from just below the knee. "Your Honor, I ask that

this item be labeled Plaintiff's B for identification."
To Jenny she said, "Is this Miss Pig Pen?"

Jenny nodded. "Yes."

"Yikes! That's a nasty cut," Heather said, looking closely at the doll. "For the record, Miss Harrison," she continued, glancing in Lindsey's direction, "the doll has its right leg removed from just below the knee. You should type that in the record." She looked across the room at Luanna. "We should have a record of what the doll looks like, right?"

"Yes, Your Honor, we should," Luanna agreed.

"You may continue, Miss Stover," Heather said to Mary Beth.

"Thank you, Your Honor."

For the next half an hour, Jenny recited experiment after experiment during which Jimmy had destroyed one toy or another. With each recitation Mary Beth produced the mangled remains of the toy. Each was described in detail for the court record. Lindsey carefully typed everything.

Phoebe sighed and leaned over to Luanna. "How much longer do you think this memorial to Jenny's toys will go on?" she whispered.

Luanna smiled and shook her head. Patience was definitely not one of Phoebe's virtues. Thankfully, a few minutes later, Mary Beth started asking Jenny about the events leading up to Rebecca's destruction.

"Miss Corbett, I'd like us to now talk about the day when your Glamour Girl doll, Rebecca, was destroyed. Did you see Mr. Corbett break your doll?"

"No, I did not."

"Then why do you think he is the one who broke it?"

"I don't *think* he broke my doll. I *know* he did!"

"Please tell the Court how you came to that conclusion," Mary Beth instructed.

"That morning I was playing with Becky in the backyard. We were having a tea party." Jenny drew in a convulsive breath and continued, "Becky loved tea parties." Tears started rolling down her face.

Heather sighed to herself.

"Anyway," Jenny continued, "there's a shed in the backyard where Jimmy creates his inventions." She rolled her eyes. "He says it's his laboratory, but really it's just an old shed Dad no longer uses. He lets Jimmy use it to store all his garbage."

"It's not garbage!" Jimmy burst out. "Those are all my scientific equipment."

"Mr. Corbett." Heather banged the gavel. "Be quiet."

Jenny continued, "He says scientific equipment, I say garbage. Whatever you want to call it, Jimmy keeps it in the shed. While Becky and I were having our tea party, Jimmy came out of the shed. He was working on another of his inventions—a glue he said would bond any type of material. When he came out of the shed, he asked me if I had any broken toys that needed fixing. He said he wanted to test his glue. I told him I didn't have any and that he should stay away from my toys. He went back into the shed muttering something about having to break something so he could fix it. Just as he went back into the shed, Mom called me inside." She paused and looked questioningly at Mary Beth.

"Please continue," Mary Beth said. "What happened next?"

"When I went to see what Mom wanted, she asked me to return a pie plate to Mrs. Cuthbert. She had given us a pie a few days earlier. On the way back, I saw you, Mary Beth, and we decided to watch a movie. I didn't remember to go back to get Becky until later that night. When I did I found her headless body lying on the ground right outside the shed door. I looked all around the yard, but I couldn't find her head anywhere." She took a deep breath and glowered at her brother. "I know he broke my doll," she declared. "He needed a broken toy to test his dumb glue, and when he couldn't find one, he broke my Becky!"

At this point Mary Beth reached into the cardboard box yet again. No one was surprised when she produced the headless body of what was obviously a Glamour Girl doll. She held up the doll and asked, "Is this your doll, Rebecca?"

"Yes, that's her," Jenny whispered.

"For the record, Your Honor, I am showing the headless body of a Glamour Girl doll to Miss Corbett. If it pleases the Court, can it be labeled Plaintiff's K for identification?"

"So ordered," Heather agreed. "Do you have any more questions for this witness?"

"No, Your Honor. I'm finished with my direct examination."

Heather looked at Luanna. "Miss Porcello, do you have any questions for Miss Corbett?"

"Yes, I do, Your Honor."

Just then Phoebe reached out and grabbed Luanna's arm. "Ask for a short break." Luanna turned to looked at her questioningly. "I want to examine the doll," Phoebe explained.

Luanna nodded her head in understanding then looked back at Heather. "Actually, Your Honor, I would like to request a brief recess."

"Very well." Heather looked at her watch. "Why don't we just adjourn until tomorrow morning?"

"That's fine, Your Honor," Luanna replied. "My investigator would like an opportunity to examine Plaintiff's K. Could you direct the bailiff to remain behind for a few minutes?" It had been decided that Jake should be in charge of any items that were entered into evidence.

"Very well," Heather said. "Bailiff, allow Miss Chen a few minutes to examine Plaintiff's K." At Jake's confused look, she sighed. "Miss Chen wants to look at the doll...the headless one." Looking around the room, she asked, "Are there any other issues that need to be taken care of?" She paused. Everyone shook his or her head in the negative. "OK, good. Court is adjourned." She banged the gavel on the table then stood and left the room.

CHAPTER 5

Crossing Jenny

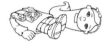

LUANNA, PHOEBE, AND Jimmy stood looking at the doll Jake had given them just a few minutes earlier.

"What are we looking for, Phoebs?" Luanna asked.

"Clues," Phoebe replied.

Luanna and Jimmy exchanged glances.

"What kind of clues?" Jimmy asked.

"I'll know when I find them." Reaching into her mini backpack, Phoebe removed a magnifying glass then proceeded to examine the doll through the lens. "There are several small indentations on the doll's body," she noted as she removed pieces of its clothing.

Jimmy and Luanna both moved closer to peer at the doll.

"Yes, I see them," Jimmy said. "And there's a small hole in the stomach. I wonder how that happened."

"I don't know," Phoebe replied thoughtfully. "That's what Luanna will have to try to find out when she questions Jenny." She looked more closely at the doll's neck where the head had been removed. Running her fingers around the edges, she said, "Someone really did rip the head off this thing. The edges are all jagged."

Luanna pondered the issue then smiled. "You're quite the investigator, Phoebs," she complimented her friend. "You've given me a direction for my cross-examination tomorrow."

❖ ❖ ❖

The following morning, once Heather had declared court was in session, Luanna proceeded to question Jennifer. "Good morning, Miss Corbett."

"Good morning," Jenny responded.

"Yesterday you recited a long list of incidents where Mr. Corbett had destroyed a number of your toys while testing his various inventions."

"Yes, I did, and that wasn't the half of it."

"Yes, but in any of those many instances did he ever deny causing the damage to the toy?"

"Well, n...no," Jenny replied hesitantly.

"So he has never once, in all the years he's been destroying your toys, denied breaking a toy when he did in fact break it?"

Jenny glared at Luanna. "I know what you're trying to do, Luanna Porcello, and I don't like it. For your information he broke those other toys before Mom and Dad told him he'd have to pay to replace any toy he destroyed, and none of them was as expensive as Becky."

"Was there a witness every time he did break a toy?" Luanna asked, ignoring Jenny's outburst.

"No, there wasn't."

"And on those times when he did break a toy and there was no eyewitness, how did you know that Mr. Corbett had been the one to break it?"

Jenny scowled at Luanna. She did not reply to the question.

"Your Honor," Luanna said, "could you please instruct the witness to answer the question?"

"Miss Corbett, answer the question, or I'll find you in contempt of court," Heather ordered. Ever since she'd assumed the role of judge for the children's court, she had spent a lot of time looking up court procedures on the Internet.

"What was the question again?" Jenny asked sulkily.

"On those times when Mr. Corbett broke a toy and there was no eyewitness, how did you know he was the one who was responsible for the damage?" Luanna repeated.

Jenny huffed then reluctantly replied, "He would admit to me that he was the one who broke it."

"In this instance with Rebecca, did he admit to removing her head from her body?"

"No, he did not. He said he didn't do it. But, like I said, Becky is way more expensive than any other toy he's broken in the past."

Addressing the Court, Luanna said, "Your Honor, if I might have Plaintiff's K, so I can ask the witness a few questions about it?"

"Yes, of course, Miss Porcello," Heather replied. "Bailiff, please give Counsel Plaintiff's K."

Jake looked confused. "Give what to who?"

Heather gritted her teeth. "Counsel. Miss Porcello. Please give her the headless doll."

"Oh. Why didn't you just say so?" Retrieving Rebecca, Jake walked over to the lectern and handed the doll to Luanna.

"Miss Corbett, is this the exact condition your doll was in when you found her lying on the ground outside the shed?" Luanna asked.

"Yes, it is."

"You haven't washed her, changed her clothes, or done anything else since you found her?" Luanna persisted.

"I did wash her," Jenny said. "She was all wet and covered with some kind of...I don't know, a kind of sticky substance."

"What color was this sticky substance?"

"It didn't have a color. It was clear, like water."

"What about her clothes? Are these the ones she was wearing on the day in question?" Luanna asked.

"No, I changed her clothes. The ones she was wearing were all dirty, and there was a rip in her shirt."

"Now, Miss Corbett, I'd like you to look closely at Rebecca's body," Luanna instructed as she walked over to the witness chair and handed the doll to Jenny. "Please describe what you see."

"There are little dent marks all over her chest, tummy, and thighs, and she has a small hole in her stomach."

"Were these marks on Rebecca before you found her lying on the ground?" Luanna asked.

"No, absolutely not!" Jenny denied vehemently. "Rebecca was in perfect condition. There wasn't a scratch on her."

"Thank you, Miss Corbett. Your Honor, I have no further questions for this witness."

"Excellent!" Heather declared. "Miss Stover, do you have any other witnesses to call?"

"Actually I do, Your Honor, but unfortunately he's at day camp and won't be available until later this afternoon. If it would be OK, can we take a break until then?"

"Just who is this witness, Miss Stover?" Heather demanded.

"It's Declan Mathias, Your Honor."

Declan Mathias? What could he possibly have to say about this situation? Luanna wondered.

"Do you have any other witness or evidence to present to the Court in the meantime?" Heather questioned. "I hate to waste an entire afternoon just waiting around." She'd read that judges were always opposed to wasting their courts' time.

"No, Your Honor, I don't," Mary Beth said apologetically. "Mr. Mathias should be available around three thirty."

"Miss Porcello, do you have anything to say about this situation?"

"The Court should ask Miss Stover to give a proffer," Luanna replied.

"Huh?" Heather queried. "What's that?"

"What I mean is, the Court should ask Miss Stover to give an offer of proof; she should give the Court some idea of what Mr. Mathias is expected to say in his testimony," Luanna explained. "To my knowledge Declan doesn't know anything about Jenny's doll being broken."

"Good point, Miss Porcello. What about it, Miss Stover? What exactly is your reason for calling Mr. Mathias to testify?"

"He's an eyewitness, Your Honor," Mary Beth replied.

"An eyewitness!" Luanna, Phoebe, and Jimmy exclaimed simultaneously.

"What's this all about, do you think?" Phoebe whispered to Luanna.

"I have no idea," Luanna whispered back. She looked at Jimmy and asked, "Do you know anything about this, Jimmy?"

"No." Jimmy looked puzzled. "I have no idea what Declan could have seen. I never touched Rebecca!"

Luanna sighed. "Well, we'll find out soon enough, I suppose."

"If there are no objections," Heather was saying, "I will adjourn court until this afternoon. We can all meet back here at three thirty. Is that acceptable to everyone?"

"Yes, Your Honor," they all agreed.

"Very well," Heather said. "Court is adjourned until three thirty."

CHAPTER 6

Caught In The Act

THAT AFTERNOON, some of the kids sat around munching on a tray of goodies Rosie had brought downstairs for them.

"Mmmm! These cookies are delicious!" Phoebe exclaimed.

"Yeah," Jake agreed. "There's no doubt Rosie makes the best cookies."

"I have to agree with you, dweeb boy," Heather said. "These are some fantastic cookies!"

Just then Mary Beth, Jenny, and Ashley walked in. A brown-skinned boy of average height accompanied them. It was Declan Mathias, the twins' next-door neighbor.

"Hey, Dec Man," Jake greeted him.

"Hey, Jake," Declan replied. "I hear you guys started a kids' court. That's pretty cool!"

"Yeah," Jake agreed. He puffed out his chest. "I'm the court's deputy." He rested his hand lightly on the butt of the toy gun that was hanging from the belt around his waist.

"Let's get started," Heather interrupted. "It's getting late." Everyone moved to take their seats. "Court is now in session," she said, banging the gavel. "Mr. Mathias, you stand here to be sworn in, then you may sit." She motioned toward the witness chair. Declan stood where she indicated. "Bailiff, please swear in the witness."

Jake strutted forward. "Raise your right hand." Declan raised his hand. "Do you promise to tell the truth, the whole truth, and nothing but the truth?" Jake asked.

"I do," Declan replied.

"Thank you, Deputy Crandall. Mr. Mathias, you may sit. Miss Stover, you may begin."

"Good afternoon, Mr. Mathias," Mary Beth said.

Declan looked amused as he replied, "Good afternoon, Miss Stover."

"Mr. Mathias, do you know my client, Jennifer Corbett, who is the plaintiff in this case?" she asked, pointing at Jenny.

"Yes, I do. She's my next-door neighbor."

"So you also know her brother, the defendant, James Corbett?"

"Yes."

"How long have you known the Corbetts?"

"About six years. I met them shortly after my family moved here."

"Would you say that you and the Corbetts are friends?" Mary Beth asked.

"I'd say we're more friendly, rather than friends. They're a couple of years behind me in school."

"Now, Mr. Mathias, let's talk about the day in question, July 5, the day Miss Corbett's doll was destroyed. Where were you that day in the late morning, early afternoon?

"I was at home."

"Did you see the defendant, James Corbett, that afternoon?"

"Yes, I did."

"When was that?"

"It was about noon. I looked out my bedroom window and saw Jimmy—Mr. Corbett—standing in his backyard."

"What was he doing?"

"He had a toy in his hand. It looked like some kind of doll. In his other hand, he had an ax."

"An ax?" she questioned. "Did you see what he did with the ax?"

"Yes. He put the toy he was holding on the chopping block, then he used the ax to hack it in half. He took one swing, and the two pieces went flying in opposite directions. It was pretty cool!"

"You're sure this occurred three days ago, on the afternoon of July 5?"

"Yes, I'm sure. It was definitely Sunday afternoon. I remember because the day before was the fourth. Besides, I have camp every day during the week, and Saturdays I have soccer practice from eleven to one, so Sunday is the only day of the week I'm home at that time of the day. I remember the time exactly because Mom had just called me down for lunch. You can set your watch by Mom's mealtimes on the weekends. Breakfast at nine, lunch at noon, dinner at five thirty—it never changes."

"Thank you, Mr. Mathias," Mary Beth looked at Heather. "I have no further questions for this witness, Your Honor."

"Excellent!" Heather exclaimed. "Things are moving along at a splendid pace. Miss Porcello, I assume you'd like to ask Mr. Mathias a few questions?"

"Yes, Your Honor, I would," Luanna replied. "However, I would like to request a short recess in order to prepare my cross-examination."

Heather looked annoyed. "How much time are we talking about, Miss Porcello? I'd really like to get this done today. You heard Declan; he has camp five days a week. That means if you don't get your cross-examination done today, we'll have to waste all day tomorrow waiting for him to come home."

"I'm sorry, Your Honor. I really do need a break; it can be a short one."

"Very well," Heather said resignedly. She banged the gavel once on her desk. "Court is in recess for fifteen minutes." She looked at Luanna. "That enough time for you, Miss Porcello?"

"Yes, thank you, Your Honor," Luanna replied. "Fifteen minutes is perfect."

❖ ❖ ❖

"What was all that about?" Phoebe demanded. Her dark eyes flashed angrily as she paced back and forth, her hair swinging furiously about her head. She stopped in front of Jimmy and eyed him balefully. She, Jimmy, and Luanna were in the

Porcellos' kitchen. The other kids had remained downstairs to finish off Rosie's cookies. "I thought you said you didn't destroy Rebecca!"

"I didn't!" Jimmy vehemently denied.

"Then what's this about Declan seeing you hack a doll to pieces?"

"He must have seen me when I cut Kid in two," he mused.

"What?" Luanna asked. "Who's Kid?"

"My Kid Kenny doll. I needed a broken toy I could use to test my glue on. I couldn't find any, so I had to break one."

"So you chopped your Kid Kenny in half?" Phoebe asked disbelievingly.

"Yes. I don't play with it anymore, so I figured it wouldn't matter if my glue didn't work and I couldn't get him back together."

"Why didn't you tell us about this from the beginning, Jimmy?" Luanna asked.

"I didn't think it was important. I mean, the issue is whether or not I broke Rebecca, and I didn't."

"I know, but now we have an eyewitness who just testified he saw you take an ax to a toy—a *doll*—on the very same day Jenny's doll had her head ripped from her body!" Luanna exclaimed. "Perhaps if you'd thought to mention this before, we would have been better prepared for this possibility." She sighed. "We'd better come up with a plan."

❖ ❖ ❖

When the trio returned to the courtroom, they were armed with a plan of action. As soon as Heather saw them approaching, she took her seat at the bench and banged the gavel. "Court is now in session," she announced. "Miss Porcello, I assume you're ready to proceed."

"I am, Your Honor. With the court's indulgence, I request that I be allowed to conduct my cross-examination onsite."

"What?" Heather asked. "I don't understand."

"I apologize, Your Honor. What I mean is, I'd like to question Mr. Mathias in his room—the place where he testified he was when he saw my client."

"Er...OK," Heather said hesitantly. "Is that OK with you, Mr. Mathias?"

"Sure," Declan readily agreed.

"OK then, let's go, everyone. We're taking the court on the road!" Heather announced. With that all the kids filed out of the courtroom.

❖ ❖ ❖

Once they all got settled in Declan's room, Luanna immediately went into her cross-examination. "Mr. Mathias, you testified that you were at home in this very room in the late morning hours of July 5. Is that correct?"

"That's right," Declan replied.

"You saw Mr. Corbett in his backyard around noon that day?"

"Yes, I did. I saw him from my bedroom window." He motioned toward the window.

Moving toward the window, Luanna looked out. "Please show the Court exactly where you saw Mr. Corbett that afternoon."

Declan moved to stand next to Luanna. Everyone except Lindsey followed. She was sitting at Declan's desk, busily typing on her laptop.

Lifting a finger, Declan pointed out the window toward Jimmy's backyard. "Right there. He was standing right there, exactly where Phoebe—I mean Miss Chen—is standing now."

All the kids looked out of the window. "Hey," Ashley cried, "why is Phoebe in Jenny's backyard?"

"Quiet!" Heather barked. She looked around, trying to find somewhere to bang her gavel. In the end she settled on the windowsill, banging the gavel several times in a row. "Please continue, Miss Porcello."

"I asked her to go over there," Luanna explained. "It will help during my cross-examination." Pulling her cell phone out of her pocket, Luanna quickly sent Phoebe a text. Then she continued questioning Declan. "Mr. Mathias, you say where Miss Chen is standing now is pretty much where you saw Mr. Corbett around noon on the fifth. Is that correct?"

"Yes."

Turning toward Heather, Luanna said, "For the record, Your Honor, Miss Chen is standing in the Corbetts' backyard, right next to the chopping block."

"So noted," Heather responded.

"Mr. Mathias, is Miss Chen holding anything in her hands?"

"Yes, she's holding a toy. A doll, I think."

"Can you tell what type of doll she's holding?"

"N-noo," Declan said hesitantly, leaning forward and squinting out the window.

"Does it resemble the toy you saw Mr. Corbett holding on the afternoon of the fifth?"

"Yes, it's pretty similar."

"Would you say it's the same toy?" Luanna enquired.

"It could be. I'm not sure." Declan leaned farther out the window. "To be honest, I wasn't paying too much attention to the toy at the time," he admitted. "I just know it was some kind of doll."

"Thank you, Mr. Mathias. Your Honor, I have no further questions for this witness."

"Excellent!" Heather exclaimed. "Miss Stover, will you be calling any other witnesses?"

"No, Your Honor," Mary Beth replied. "The plaintiff rests."

"You're tired?" Jake asked disbelievingly.

"No, Jake." Luanna laughed. "Mary Beth means she's done with her case. She has no more witnesses or evidence to bring to court."

"If we're done with the vocabulary lesson," Heather interjected, "let's get on with it. Will you be ready to proceed with your case in the morning, Miss Porcello?" she asked.

"Yes, Your Honor, I'll be ready," Luanna announced.

"Very good," Heather said. "Court is adjourned until tomorrow morning."

CHAPTER 7

Jimmy Comes Clean

LUANNA LAY IN her bed, staring up at the ceiling. Her mind was totally preoccupied with Jimmy's case. *Is he really as innocent as he claims he is?* she wondered. *Is he lying? He does have a really good reason to lie—Glamour Girl dolls are very, very expensive.*

There was a quiet knock at her door before Renee Porcello peeked in. "May I come in?"

Luanna looked over at her mom and smiled. "Of course."

"I came to tuck you in."

Luanna rolled her eyes. "I'm not a baby, Mom," she protested. "I'll be eleven in less than a month!"

"You'll always be my baby," Mrs. Porcello said as she smoothed down Luanna's sheets. "What's wrong?"

Luanna frowned. "What makes you think anything is wrong?"

"You pull your hair only when you're upset, anxious, or preoccupied with something. And right now you're about to twist that braid right off of your head."

Luanna looked self-consciously at the long, dark-brown braid she had twisted around her finger. She sighed. "Nothing is wrong. Not really. I was just thinking. Mary Beth finished Jenny's case today, so now it's my turn to present Jimmy's side. I've been lying here racking my brain trying to think of a way to prove he's innocent."

"Well, that's your first mistake."

Luanna furrowed her brow in confusion. "What do you mean?"

"You're forgetting one of the basic principles of law," her mother explained. "It's the plaintiff's job to prove the defendant's guilt, not the defendant's job to prove his innocence."

"You're right, of course," Luanna said. "I even told Jimmy that very same thing at the beginning of the case, when he asked me how he could prove his

innocence. But somehow, I lost sight of that truth."
She sighed again. "I guess I got so caught up in the
excitement of defending my first client, I just
forgot." She looked sheepishly at her mother.

"Don't be embarrassed about that," Mrs. Porcello
said. "I've been there many a time myself—especially
at the beginning of my career. But the fact is,
innocent or not, our clients deserve vigorous
defenses."

"What if Jimmy really did destroy Jenny's doll?
What then? How do I defend him?"

"As a defense lawyer, one of your best strategies
is to poke holes in the plaintiff's case. You try to
show why any evidence they present is not reliable
or why it could just as easily point to someone else's
guilt. You want to point your jury—or, in this case,
your judge—in another direction. Get them to view
the evidence in a light that is favorable to your
client."

"I think I understand," Luanna said slowly. "Even
if Jimmy is guilty, I make them fight to prove it. But
what if he's innocent? He says he is, but there's a lot
of evidence that makes him look bad, if not
downright guilty."

"Do you believe him?"

Luanna hesitated then said in a firm voice, "Yes, I do. I had my doubts for a moment, but I know Jimmy. He would never lie. Not even to get out of trouble."

"Well, then," Mrs. Porcello said, "maybe you should review the evidence to see if it points to the identity of the real perpetrator."

"What?"

"There's a good chance some of the evidence that's been presented in court points to the identity of the real guilty party. After all, one thing that is for certain is that the doll was destroyed. Someone had to have done it."

"Mom, you're a genius!" Luanna exclaimed. "Look for clues to the real perpetrator. Why didn't I think of that?"

Renee Porcello laughed. "Genius? No, never that. But I have been doing this for a very long time. Remember, it's only your first foray into the world of trial law, so give yourself a break." She leaned over and kissed Luanna on the cheek. "Don't stay up too late. You'll need to be fresh and alert if you're going to start presenting Jimmy's side of the case tomorrow."

"Good night, Mom," Luanna replied. "And thanks."

"Good night, baby."

❖ ❖ ❖

The next morning Luanna, Phoebe, and Jimmy were all sitting around the defense table in the courtroom. The three friends had agreed to meet early to discuss strategy before Luanna began presenting Jimmy's case in court.

"So that's the plan," Luanna said. "We're going to try to poke holes in the evidence they've presented so far."

"Declan's eyewitness testimony is a bit hard to refute," Phoebe said.

"I actually thought Luanna did a great job undermining his testimony," Jimmy said. "Sure, he saw me take an ax to a doll, but he couldn't even say what type of doll it was, much less that it was Rebecca. And I'll testify it was Kid Kenny."

"True," Luanna agreed. "And he even admitted the doll Phoebe was holding—your Kid Kenny doll—resembled the actual doll he saw you chopping on Sunday. By the way, that glue of yours is amazing! Your Kid Kenny doll is almost as good as new."

"Thanks. But it's not as good as I thought it would be. It works only on paper and—"

"That all sounds good," Phoebe interrupted, "but you've got to admit, it's quite a coincidence that on the very day Jimmy decides to hack a doll in two, his *sister's* doll turns up missing its head!"

"You're right," Luanna agreed, "but all we can do is try our best to show the weaknesses in the evidence. Also, don't forget, my mom said we should reexamine all the evidence to see if it points to the real perpetrator."

"Hmm..." Phoebe paused, mentally reviewed all the evidence that had been presented in court so far, and then said, "I can't see how any of it points to any one particular person."

"We'll just have to wait and see how things develop," Luanna responded. "In the meantime, Jimmy, was there anyone else–?"

Just then Mary Beth, Jenny, and Ashley walked into the courtroom, putting an end to any further private discussion.

"Hey, guys," they all greeted as they moved across the room to where the trio sat.

"Hey," Phoebe, Luanna, and Jimmy replied.

Within minutes the other kids arrived. Almost immediately, Heather called the court to order. "Miss Porcello, are you ready to begin?"

"I am, Your Honor."

"Very good. You may proceed."

"I call James Corbett to the stand," Luanna announced. Once Jimmy took the witness chair and Deputy Jake duly swore him in, Luanna began her examination.

"Mr. Corbett, you were present when the plaintiff, your sister, testified about the numerous times in the past that you've broken her toys. Do you admit to all the incidents she recounted in court?"

"Yes, I do. Well, all except for Rebecca. I did not break Rebecca."

"Miss Corbett testified that on the day in question, you were working on a new invention in your shed. Tell us about that morning."

"I was working on creating a new type of glue. I was hoping to produce one that would bond any type of material: fabric, wood, plastic, acrylic—anything. Anyway, I had gotten to the point where I was ready to test it, but I needed something to test it on. I couldn't find anything in the shed, so I went outside to take a look around the yard. That's when I saw Jenny having a tea party with her doll, Rebecca. I asked her if she had any broken toys, but she said she didn't."

"What did you do then?"

"I went back into the shed for a moment. When I came back outside, Jenny was gone. I went inside the house to see if I could find anything I could use to test my glue on. I couldn't find anything broken, so when I came across my old Kid Kenny doll buried in the bottom of my toy box, I decided to use him instead. I fetched the ax from the garage, went back into the backyard, and used the ax to cut Kid in two. That must have been when Declan saw me."

"Think back, Mr. Corbett. Does anything about that day stand out to you?"

Jimmy carefully considered her question then said, "No, everything seemed normal. Mom was busy in the kitchen baking a batch of brownies for a charity bake sale. Dad was out golfing with Colin." He chuckled. "Dad says he's determined that at least one of his children will share his love for the game, and since neither Jenny nor I care for it, he's now focusing all his efforts on Colin. Anyway, it was a typical Sunday; everyone was doing their usual thing." He smiled. "Well, all except for Rufus. He was having a lazy Sunday. Usually he's off somewhere getting into trouble, but that day he was just lying around napping."

"Rufus?" Luanna asked. "You mean Mrs. Cuthbert's dog?"

"Yes," Jimmy replied. "He spends a lot of time at our house. Poor Mrs. Cuthbert is too old to deal with him, so my parents volunteered to have Jenny and me help take care of him. He has a few bad habits, but he's really a very sweet dog."

Reaching into a canvas bag she had brought to court, Luanna pulled out a doll. "Your Honor, I ask that this item be marked as Defense 1 for identification."

"So ordered," Heather replied.

"Thank you, Your Honor. Mr. Corbett, do you recognize Defense 1?"

"I do," he replied. "It's my Kid Kenny doll."

"Is this the Kid Kenny doll you say you cut...?" Luanna frowned. *Review the evidence, and see who else it could point to. Who else?* she wondered.

"Miss Porcello, is there a problem?" Heather's voice interrupted Luanna's thoughts.

"Um, no, Your Honor. I'm sorry, I just had a thought. I'll continue."

"Please do," Heather said.

"I'm sorry, Mr. Corbett. As I was saying, is this the Kid Kenny doll you cut in half on Sunday?" Luanna asked.

"Yes, it is."

Who else? Who else? Luanna's thoughts were spinning around in her head.

"Miss Porcello?" Heather said.

"Hmm?"

"Would you care to continue?" Heather asked.

"Er, yes, sorry, Your–" *Buried...That's it!* "Your Honor, could I have a brief recess?" Luanna asked excitedly.

"You're acting very strangely, Miss Porcello." Heather frowned. "I guess a short recess would be OK," she said resignedly. "How much time do you need?"

"Maybe we could reconvene after lunch? Oh, and if we could meet at Phoebe's–I mean Miss Chen's–house, that would be great!"

The other kids were all staring wide eyed at Luanna.

"I think she's lost her mind," Mary Beth whispered to Jenny. "The strain of trying to prove Jimmy innocent must have gotten to her."

Phoebe looked across to where Mary Beth sat at the plaintiff's table. "I think you're about to lose your case, Mary Beth," she said, a smug look on her face. She knew Luanna well enough to know that whenever she seemed distracted, it usually meant she was on to something.

While this exchange was taking place, Heather declared the court in recess. They were to meet back at Phoebe's house after lunch.

Luanna walked over to where Phoebe sat "Let's go, Phoebs."

"What's going on, Luanna?" Jenny demanded.

Luanna smiled. "You'll see," she said mysteriously.

CHAPTER 8

Digging For The Truth

THAT AFTERNOON, all the kids stood around in Phoebe's backyard, waiting to get started.

"This is highly irregular, Miss Porcello," Heather grumbled. "Court is in session," she added irritably. She looked helplessly around for somewhere to bang her gavel, finally settling her gaze on Jake's head. He eyed her warily, and moved back a few paces out of her reach. Heather sighed. "You may begin, Miss Porcello."

"Thank you, Your Honor. If you would all follow Miss Chen," Luanna said as Phoebe started walking toward the conservation land next door.

"Where are we going?" Mary Beth asked.

"If I'm right, everything will become clear soon enough," Luanna replied.

After several minutes Phoebe came to a halt. "Here we are," she announced. She motioned toward a mound of dirt that looked like it had been recently disturbed. "This is it."

"You're up, Jimmy," Luanna said.

Jimmy took the shovel he was carrying and started digging into the mound. After a couple of minutes, he felt the shovel hit against something. "I think I've found it!" he exclaimed and started digging faster. After he'd removed another couple shovelfuls of dirt, he stopped and looked into the hole he'd dug. "Wow!"

Everyone moved closer so they could get a better look. In the hole they could see a small pile of various items.

"Hey, that's my journal!" Mary Beth exclaimed. "I've been looking all over for that." She pointed to a small, leather-bound book, all tattered and covered with dirt, which lay on the top of the heap.

"Actually you weren't looking all over for it," Ashley said. "You accused *me* of taking it."

While the girls were arguing, Luanna stooped down in the shallow opening and sifted through the collection of things. As she picked up each item, she briefly examined it before tossing it aside. Finally, she shouted triumphantly, "Here it is!" She raised her hand, waving the object she was holding back and forth.

"Ew!" Mary Beth said. "What is that?"

Luanna brushed off some of the dirt and moved aside the clumps of matted hair that were covering the object. Before she had completed the task, Jenny screeched, "It's Rebecca's head!" She looked confused. "I don't understand; what is it doing *here*?"

"Perhaps you'd like to explain, Miss Porcello," Heather suggested.

"I'd be happy to, Your Honor."

"Ooh, this is like a Perry Mason moment!" Mary Beth said excitedly.

"Who's Perry Mason?" Jake asked. "Is he in our class?"

"No, Jake," Ashley answered. "He's an amazing lawyer in an old television courtroom drama." She looked around at all the blank faces. "Oh, never mind. It's not important. Let's listen to what Luanna has to say."

Luanna smiled. "Thanks, Ashley," she said and then proceeded with her explanation. "From the very beginning, I was focused on the wrong aspect of this case. I was determined to prove Jimmy's innocence. In doing so I forgot one of the main principles of law: the *plaintiff* has the burden of proof, not the defendant. I got so caught up in trying to disprove Jenny's case, I forgot to ask the one question I should have asked from the very beginning: if not Jimmy, then *who*? If Jimmy is truly innocent—and I believe he is——then *someone else* destroyed Rebecca. We all know how much Jenny loves Rebecca, so she obviously didn't do it. But the only other person who had access to the doll was Jimmy. *Or was he?* I'm ashamed to say I didn't even stop to consider who else it could have been until I had a talk with my mom. She advised me to reexamine the evidence, not only to find its weaknesses, but also to see if it pointed to the identity of the real perpetrator. That's when I started to review the evidence in my head. Immediately, I realized there had been clues to the identity of the real culprit from the very beginning." She looked at Jake. "Jake, could I please have Rebecca's body?"

Jake pulled the doll from the backpack he carried and handed it to her. At Luanna's suggestion he had brought the doll along on the court's impromptu road trip.

"Thanks." Removing the doll's clothing, Luanna pointed to the body. "Remember these indentations all over the chest, stomach, and thighs? Phoebe pointed them out the first time we examined the doll, but we couldn't figure out what could have caused them. Then there's this puncture wound in the tummy." She touched a finger to the jagged hole in the doll's stomach. "Those were the first clues that someone other than Jimmy had committed the crime. Why would Jimmy put dents in the doll if all he wanted to do was test his glue on it? The answer is, he wouldn't. But there was Declan's testimony to contend with. He said he saw Jimmy chop a doll in two. Of course he couldn't say *which* doll Jimmy had taken the ax to, but the implication that it was Rebecca was there.

"However, if you believe that the doll Declan saw Jimmy cutting in two was Rebecca, then you have to explain how it is that Rebecca has these jagged marks around her neck." Again she lifted the doll's body, this time pointing to the marks about the neck area where the head had been removed. "Remember, Declan said he saw Jimmy take 'one swing, and the two pieces went flying in opposite directions.' These marks were obviously not caused by a single blow of an ax. They are too jagged and uneven. Arguably, a single blow from an ax would leave smoother cut lines. But then, there was another problem for Jimmy: his long history of destroying toys. True, he had never denied breaking a toy in the past–even when there was no eyewitness–but that was *before* his parents decided he would have to pay to replace any toy he was responsible for breaking. And as Jenny pointed out in her testimony, none of those toys had been nearly as expensive as Rebecca. It's a powerful reason to lie, and I admit that for a moment–a very brief moment–I started to doubt Jimmy. Yet in the end, I couldn't bring myself to believe he would lie. It's just not in his character.

"So this brings me back to the original question: if not Jimmy, then *who*? It came to me during Jimmy's testimony. He said he'd found his Kid Kenny doll buried in the bottom of his toy chest. *Buried.* That's when it hit me! There was someone else in the yard that day, someone who has a habit of taking people's stuff and running off with it–someone who has a habit of *burying* the things that he steals!"

All the kids looked bewilderedly at one another–well, all except Phoebe and Jimmy. They knew exactly to whom Luanna was referring.

"I'm talking about Rufus," Luanna declared. "*He* is the one who has been snatching people's stuff in the neighborhood. Jimmy testified Rufus was in the backyard with him on Sunday afternoon. Jenny testified she left Rebecca sitting at the tea table when she went on an errand for her mother. Rebecca was within easy reach for Rufus. He likes to chew on things, hence the indentations and the puncture wound on Rebecca's body. Then there's the fact that Jenny said when she found Rebecca's body, it was wet and covered with a clear substance that was kind of sticky. Dogs' saliva is somewhat sticky. Put it all together, and it makes sense.

"I figured if Rufus had removed the head, then most likely he would have buried it somewhere. I remembered Phoebe telling me she'd chased him down to his burial site when he took off with her sister's flute. Typically, dogs have favorite holes they use over and over, so the chances were that if he'd buried Rebecca's head, he had buried it in the same spot where he'd attempted to bury Penelope's flute. So Phoebe, Jimmy, and I came out here to look for Rufus's hole. Phoebe had a pretty good idea of where it was from her previous run-in with him. Once we found it, I decided it would be best to bring you all out here, so you could witness for yourselves where Rebecca's head has been hidden all this time."

Just then Rufus came barreling out from among the trees, headed in their direction. In his mouth he carried a baseball glove. As soon as he saw them, he stopped.

Jenny scowled and shouted, "Bad dog, Rufus!"

Rufus whined and dropped the glove on the ground. Prominently printed on it were the letters "JC."

"Hey, that's my baseball glove!" Jake exclaimed.

Everyone burst out laughing.

"Well, that clinches it," Heather declared. "You can't argue with the facts. So, if there are no objections, Miss Stover," she said, looking at Mary Beth, "I intend to find in favor of the defense."

Mary Beth looked at Jenny. Jenny shook her head and said, "I have no objection. Obviously Rufus is the real culprit." She sighed and looked at her brother. "I'm sorry I didn't believe you, Jimmy. I guess I was so upset about losing Rebecca, I lost my head. Can you ever forgive me?"

"Don't give it another thought," Jimmy said to his twin.

"We have no objections, Your Honor," Mary Beth said.

"Very good," Heather said. "It is the opinion of this Court that the defendant is innocent of the claim against him. And let this be a lesson to you, Miss Corbett. It's never good to jump to conclusions without having all the facts. OK, we're done here. Bailiff, you may return the items of evidence to their respective owners. Court is adjourned." Reaching behind her, she banged the gavel on a tree trunk for emphasis. "Nice work, everyone."

So it wasn't Jimmy after all, Lindsey thought, shaking her head in disbelief. All through the proceedings, she'd been sitting quietly, busily typing on her computer. *All this work for nothing!* She sighed.

"Don't worry, Jen," Jimmy was saying to his sister. "We'll find a way to replace Rebecca. I've got some savings. Maybe we can pool our money together and convince Mom and Dad to chip in."

"It's really good of you to offer, Jimmy, especially after all I put you through. But Rebecca was one of a kind, you know? She can never be replaced. I'll just have to be happy with my memories of her."

❖ ❖ ❖

A little while later, after all the other kids had left, Luanna, Heather, and Phoebe stood outside in the Chens' front yard. The three girls were discussing the outcome of the case.

"Who would have thought," Heather said, "that the dog did it?"

"Well, I for one was not surprised," Phoebe declared. "I've always known that Rufus is a menace to society!"

Luanna giggled. Just then, they noticed two boys walking up the street toward them. They were pulling along a badly beaten-up go-kart between them. It was Declan Mathias and Greg Foster. As the boys approached, the girls could hear them arguing.

"I didn't cause the accident, Greg. I'm telling you, there's something wrong with the go-kart!" Declan declared.

"There's absolutely nothing wrong with the go-kart," Greg shot back. "You lost control when you jerked the steering wheel too hard."

"I did not!"

As the two boys continued to argue back and forth, Heather sighed and put her arms around Luanna and Phoebe's shoulders. "Looks like court will need to be in session again, ladies—and soon!"

BOOK TWO AVAILABLE SOON!

Luanna and The Kids' Court #2
The Go-KartAstrophe

GREG FOSTER IS furious with his best friend, Declan Mathias, after Declan crashes and destroys his prized go-kart. Now Greg can't achieve his lifelong dream of entering the annual Tri-County Go-Kart Race-a-Thon! Greg demands that Declan pay for the damages, but Declan refuses, insisting he's not to blame for the accident. When Greg takes his case to the kids' court, can Luanna once again work her magic, solve the case, and save the boys' friendship?

AUTHOR'S NOTE

Thank you so much for reading *The Doll Dilemma*! It's the first book in what will hopefully be a long and fruitful series. I really hope you enjoyed reading it as much as I enjoyed writing it. Please take the time to leave a review at Amazon. Not only can reader reviews be helpful to authors, but they are also a great way to help other readers discover new books.

If you liked *The Doll Dilemma,* then keep an eye out for book two in the Luanna and The Kids' Court series, *The Go-KartAstrophe*, which will be released soon. If you want to make sure you don't miss any future releases, sign up for my newsletter at caronpescatore.com. You can also connect with me at http://facebook.com/caron.pescatore, or at https://twitter.com/LuannaKidsCourt.

ABOUT THE AUTHOR

CARON PESCATORE was born in the United Kingdom. She spent most of her childhood in Jamaica, before migrating to the United States. After practicing as a registered nurse for many years, she decided to enter the field of law, obtaining her J.D. in 2001. She worked as an attorney for a number of years, before leaving the profession to become a stay-at-home mom—her most challenging career to date. Ms. Pescatore is passionate about justice and fairness for all; a sentiment which led, in part, to her decision to write the Luanna and The Kids' Court series. Her favorite pastimes are reading, writing, and watching true-crime shows.

She also recently discovered a love of painting using stencils. At present, Ms. Pescatore lives in Massachusetts with her husband and family.

CPSIA information can be obtained at www.ICGtesting.com
Printed in the USA
BVOW02s2050140616

452067BV00008B/27/P